How to Build the Perfect Cat Fence
with Sheila Shaw

NOTES

PLEASE NOTE: Due to the variability of materials, skills, and manufacturing differences, the publisher and author assume no responsibility for any personal injury, property damage, pet injury, or other loss of any sort suffered from any actions taken based on or inspired by information or advice herein. Make sure you completely understand any procedure before beginning work. If ever uncertain, consult a professional handyperson.

ISBN: 978-1-6319203-6-3

Three Gals Publishing, Monterey, California
www.ThreeGalsPublishing.com

Three Gals Publishing
inspiring genius

DEDICATION

This book is dedicated to all the people who value our four-legged friends and see them not just as pets, but as, if I may stretch a bit, Our Spiritual Equals.

To Zoe, whose journey with me was all too brief, and to Prince, my little Min Pin, who at the time of writing this book passed away at age eighteen and a half. He blessed me with his friendship, love, loyalty and most of all his PRESENCE. Thank you, and may the Source be with All of Us.

BOOK CONTENTS

DVD CONTENTS

Title	Description
My Inspiration	Brief explanation of why I built my fence showing 360° bird's-eye view of yard enclosed
Tour	Tour of my yard, my plan and my challenges
Post /Rebar 1 & 2	Tutorial of how to bend the rebar and set the post
Fencing	Tutorial on how to place the fencing
Finished	The completed fence
The Escape	Rocky and Boogie escape after 21 days and how they did it
2014 Updates	As the years have passed, modifications have been made
Bonus	Strategic sign placement of how I recovered my neighbor's missing puppy lost in the forest

ACKNOWLEDGMENTS

I especially thank The Divine Source for giving me the talent to build and the conscience to share. Peggi Speers, my very best friend, whose light never dims and encouragement forever grows. My sister Jeannie Shaw, who has literally given me life (kidney) and whose encouragement is only rivaled by Peggi's. Sharon Law-Tucker, for her great wisdom and many funny sayings that send me into a deep belly laugh for days on end. Mary Margaret Rose, whom I miss so dearly, I look forward to seeing you again, my beautiful friend. Debbie Miller for your kind gentle heart. Christine LePorte for doing an awesome job editing. And last but not least, my little Min Pin, Prince, who generously shared his home with all the cats when he was first.

FAIR WARNING

Before embarking on this task, I must offer you fair warning that you may soon develop a slight heartache. At least for those of us who used to allow our cats out to roam the neighborhood anyway. When you see them sitting at the fence looking as though they miss their freedom you can't help but to wonder if there is a club they used to belong to or a girlfriend or boyfriend they'd visit on a daily basis. It gets me the most when they look at you with those huge marble eyes as though to study you, wondering what happened, and know you are the responsible party for this dramatic change. Of course they will continue to love you for allowing them to go outside and stretch their little paws, for feeding them top of the line organic cat food, keeping their bedding clean and yes, litter boxes too, and the biggest one is for not bringing any more supposed playmates home. I'm not too sure cats like sharing their home with other cats, at least after they grow up anyway.

Due to this new, what seems to be prison, they could develop a somewhat distant relationship with you for not allowing them to roam the neighborhood and prove their "meow hood" if it's a boy, and the occasional "I don't want to live with you anymore and I'm gonna move next door" if it's a girl. However, on the bright side of things, every night you can close your eyes knowing your loving four-legged—in my case 24-legged—feline family will survive another day against the combat of four-wheeled machines and the wild animals that prey on them, and our feline friends will be safe yet another day to love.

If you have decided you can adapt to this possible heartache, read on, my friends, it gets better. And welcome to the "I like to think I am in control of my cats" club. LOL

Caution: Don't think after a while your cats will get accustomed to the idea they cannot leave the yard and stop looking for ways to do so. Boogie, aka Houdini, never stops looking for a way out. Once your fence is complete make it a daily practice to walk the fence line and look for any breaches, especially if your fence is like mine and is in the forest. If other animals are used to coming into your yard, such as skunks and raccoons, they will still try to get back in, at least initially.

MY INSPIRATION

On July 28, 2009, my day began in the ritualistic way it always does. At 6:00 a.m. my left eye opens as the dawn peeks through my window. Not quite ready to get up, I roll over, turn up my heated blanket, and just as I am settling in again, I hear the notorious halfhearted bark from my Min Pin alerting me it's time to go to the bathroom, immediately followed by his much awaited breakfast.

Not wanting to get up, I attempt to sneak him out the back door quietly, trying desperately not to wake the other six four-legged residents that reside in my busy household. Too late! As the brisk morning fresh air hits his nose, his halfhearted bark has turned into a full-blown wake-up call to the rest of the clan, aggressively announcing, "Breakfast is being served!" Ugh, no rolling over at this point, it is time to start the day.

As I roll out of bed, my Min Pin encourages me to hurry up and serve breakfast. At this point, my six cats, which are not nearly as aggressive as my Min Pin, slowly arrive to breakfast, stretching and yawning as they all sit in their designated feeding areas.

Before I get too deep into this story, I should give you a brief but clear description of my six cats and their personalities. Believing 100 percent that cats are not of this world and much more intelligent than most humans—at least me anyway—I wasn't surprised when they completely organized who sits where at breakfast. The only thing I had to do was obey their will, and, of course, feel very privileged to serve them and be in their presence.

Meet the pride:

1) Zoe is the high priestess who in a past life must have been the Queen of the Nile. She is a solid black long-haired cat who insists on eating in a separate room and will not share a litter box with any of the other cats. She also has to have her bedding changed every few days.

2) Niles, a short-haired solid black cat, is absolutely a sweetie with a very "manly disposition," if this is even possible for a cat. He is also extremely verbal and always has to know what is going on. However, he is the first one to scurry off to safety whenever he senses a different energy in the house. Niles is also very sensitive and developed a food allergy to gluten and grain, which had a side effect on him that showed up as aggressive behavior, later discussed in the section "Food for Thought."

3) Rocky—for those of you who have seen the movie *Rocky*, if Rocky Balboa was a cat this is definitely what he would be like. Everybody loves Rocky. He is a short-haired tiger cat who is built like a mountain lion. Rocky's personality is equaled to a surfer boy who spends his afternoons indulging in some sort of illegal party substance. His eyes are always drooped and he has a very mellow disposition. At least that's what I always thought. I heard a different story when Boogie went missing and when I was talking to my neighbors looking for her, I learned Rocky was truly "Rocky" as he was picking fights with other male cats. Yikes, how embarrassing.

4) Boogie—now Boogie is absolutely gorgeous. She is a little Maine Coon! I do not say this as if I am some sort of Maine Coon expert. The truth is I only found out she is a Maine Coon when a friend was over and told me. I always thought she was a mutt since I trapped her along with Rocky and Jasper when they were kittens. Boogie is also known as "The Great Houdini." I say this with much emphasis. If there is a way out, she will find it. Bar none, she is the smartest cat I own.

5) Jasper, aka Little Jay/JJ/Left Eye, is your classic tuxedo cat with a splash of white on his nose, and a white chest and feet. He is the baby of the bunch and the last one I trapped. When he was a kitten a predator got to him causing his right eye to look like it has a permanent cataract because whatever got him must have scratched his eye. Oh, but don't feel bad, he sees perfectly well, especially when he wants to take a poke at Casey. His own mother, for crying out loud, geez! He is totally mellow until he goes outside, when he reverts to a wild cat. Don't get me wrong, JJ is a total lover, he just has a rather funny relationship with his mother. Can anyone shed some light on what this is all about?

6) Casey; now if it was not for Casey, I would not have Rocky, Boogie and Jasper as she is the mama. Casey's story is unique and deserves to be told, so please bear with me as I tell it. Casey was this beautiful white and tan kitten about 6 months old that came out of nowhere at the business park where I had an office.

The business park was located in a country atmosphere and was safe for stray cats. I used to say to my co-workers, if I were a cat, I would come here. I mean we had this great country restaurant that served the best bacon, eggs and grits. Wait, what am I saying, cats don't eat eggs!

Every now and again a new kitten would pop up and then disappear. However, Casey was different as she would hang around my office door. Every day I would look out the window and she would be close by, so I started feeding her and made a little food shelter so the food would not get wet from the morning dew. I hated leaving her at the end of the day as I felt she was destined to be in my life and I in hers. It's amazing I even got any work done in the three months from the time she showed up until I moved. After a month had passed and she was still around, I decided I would try to trap her and take her home. So, I got a trap and checked it every two hours, as my office was only 2 miles from my home. Yes, I am one of those kooks who will actually get up in the middle of the night because if I caught her, I did not want her to spend too much time in the trap.

The next morning, around 6 a.m., there in the trap was this tiny tiger kitten, now called Rocky! I can't tell you how shocked I was. Not only was there a kitten in the trap, but two more to boot! While Rocky was in the trap there were two other kittens, Boogie and Jasper, outside the trap looking at him chowin' down all the food, and when they caught sight of me, they split like a log; okay maybe not a log, but like lightning for sure. You've probably guessed by now, Casey had kittens!!! Uggggh.

I took Rocky home and contemplated what I was going to do with him. I was torn because I couldn't keep him and not keep the others. I was moving to a new home and would have plenty of room for all of them, so I decided to keep him, and if I could catch the others, them too!

I was able to catch Boogie while she was dead asleep on top of a post and Jasper on another. Jasper immediately woke up and darted off when he saw me. He split so fast, he didn't even bother to warn Boogie. Geez, some big brother he made! Since Boogie did not hear me, I was able to pick her up without warning. Awesome, two down, two to go!

Once again I set the trap. Poor little one-eyed Jasper could not resist the food and after three days, in he went. Yippee. Now all I needed was Casey, and at this point, I was getting worried I would not get her in time as I was moving in just one week. There was no way she was getting in the trap, especially after seeing two of her kittens get it. She would not deny herself the food, however; she was digging under the trap and spooning the food out using her paw. So now, not only could I not get her in the trap, but now she was not hungry.

With the office packed and the U-Haul standing by, I was sick with fear I would be leaving her behind. I decided to go have one last dinner at the country restaurant with a friend. After our meal, we stood in the parking lot; at this time it was well past daylight and empty. We placed a long prayer, asking the angels to help us catch her. Immediately, we came up with the idea to place a dish of food just inside my office door with my friend standing behind it and out of sight. The plan was to slam the door shut when Casey walked in to get the irresistible food. This sounded like a great plan. I planted the food just inside the door with my friend behind it and started walking back to my cubicle, when suddenly the door slammed and scared the daylights out of me. I turned around and said, "What in the world did you do that for?" I mean, I had barely taken 5 steps, if that! My friend looked at me with wide eyes, pointing her finger as if to say look, and there Casey was, trapped in my office!

7)   Prince (honorable mention), aka "The Doo," "Papa," "Mr. Eat Everybody's Food When They're Not Looking," and "The Boss Over Everyone." I can't say enough about Prince. He was sweet, friendly, happy, fun, funny, loving, cute, and everything Heaven represents and when he passed away, March 15th, 2014, after 18½ years, it was as if my heart was torn right out of me. Until I looked up and saw my 5 cats (Zoe has since passed) looking back at me as if to say, he is safe, so let's you and I play and continue our journey. May the Great Source bless our animals and those of us who love them.

After breakfast, before letting them out, I remind them that all the winged and crawling critters have a right to live too and unless they are absolutely starving or in a position of self-defense, to let them live to see another day and not wind up in their already over-filled bellies. I tell them to watch out for cars, don't go into anyone's house or garage where they could get possibly trapped, I love them, to check in every few hours, and last but not least, to be home by or before curfew. Which is 5 o'clock SHARP! And off they go! As they set sail for their daily adventure, I couldn't help but to wonder if this will be the last time I see them; this thought always left me with an unsettling feeling in my stomach. Living in the forest can be very dangerous for cats, between the many mountain lions, wild dogs and who knows what else. It's this thought that keeps me on my toes to stick with curfew with no exceptions!

Every evening at 4:30 I start reeling them in. I go out in the middle of the street and yell each one of their names to be sure I am heard. It's Rocky's name that I must yell the loudest as he tends to travel the farthest. My neighbor told me every evening at this time she starts to sing the *Rocky* theme song. LOL. I should mention she did not seem too happy about it either. I repeat this process every fifteen minutes and by 5 p.m. they are all here.

Except this evening was different: no Boogie. Even though this was not the first time someone was late for curfew, I had that sick feeling in my stomach that something was wrong. After 8 p.m. rolled around and still no Boogie, it seemed that nothing else mattered but finding my beautiful cat. Since my imagination is very colorful and wild, panic became the dominant emotion. By morning, I went into full combat mode and loaded up my backpack with fliers and 4x4 leaflets and went door to door covering 3 square miles. (*See section* RECOVER YOUR LOST PET USING STRATEGIC SIGN PLACEMENT.)

I had been living in the forest at this point for 3 years and for the most part was a stranger to most of my neighbors. However, by the end of the day, I knew all of them and they knew me. They invited me in and shared how they saw my cat(s) on a daily basis and even gave me details on the routes they would take. Some of the details were a bit TMI, crossing streets going into the green belt. Yipes, now I was really sick; she could be anywhere. This is when it became apparent to me I would build that cat fence I had been considering.

So, you ask, what happened to Boogie? Mark, my neighbor, would come up on the weekends as this was his second home, and work on the remodeling. Boogie, expressing her curious nature, slipped into his garage when he was not looking, and when he left she was closed in and trapped. She was trapped for 3 nights and 4 days. Funny, here I was trekking all around the neighborhood and here she was next door the entire time. When he returned a few days later, she made her escape.

NOTES

GETTING STARTED

Note: If you choose to hire a person to build the fence for you, be sure to read this book and watch the DVD in their entirety yourself before handing the task to someone else. Do not let them take any shortcuts; monitor them closely and be sure they are following this guideline step-by-step. Of course, there are always improvements and alternative ways to do any task. However, stick close to what I am offering, as I have thought this process out very well and proven it to be successful. In other words, stick with what works!

When designing my cat fence I did not know what to expect. I didn't even know if it was going to work. After all, I had never built anything even close to this. I did not know if my cats would try to climb it, get on top of it, chew it or even dig under it. Therefore, I took all of the extra precautions just in case they did any one of the above. However, when all was said and done, even until this day, they didn't do any of the things I just mentioned.

Why did I wait 5 years to write this book? When building something as important as a cat fence, and especially if you plan to encourage others to do the same, you'd better be sure not only does it work, but it continues to work over a period of time as well. Cats are clever and never stop looking for ways to escape, at least those who are accustomed to exploring your neighborhood. Over the past 5 years I have been fortunate to only have a few minor incidents that were easily corrected. I am confident in writing this book at this time and confident my information is well researched and proven to be successful.

I strongly recommend you watch the entire DVD first, as this will give you a good idea on how to approach your project and what steps you need to take and when to take them. However, I strongly recommend not trying to build the fence from the DVD alone. At the time I was recording the building of my fence there were things I did or said that I later went back and changed or learned to be different. Please also read this book, and together the two will help you avoid making any unnecessary mistakes. I also encourage you to watch each DVD section more than once. This will familiarize you with specific tasks, so when you start, it will be as if you have already done it.

TOOLS AND SUPPLIES

When putting this tool list together, my goal was to be as thorough as possible to be sure you will be totally prepared and successful. Therefore, once you get started you will have everything you need to complete the project without having to stop and run to the hardware store, as I did more times than I care to count! Many of the tools listed here will hopefully already be in your arsenal of tools. However, before going out and buying any tools you feel you will only use once for this project, consider borrowing them from a friend, and if that is not possible, consider a garage sale or your local swap meet; these are great places to get top-notch tools for bargain prices. Just be sure before getting started you have EVERYTHING listed here—you will need it all.

With that in mind, I always say, if you need it once, you will need it again. Also, once you are successful in building your cat fence, trust me, you will be encouraged to do more projects yourself and tools are the key!

Please note: The prices listed are based on one of the larger home improvement centers and may vary. Additionally, I used the lowest price, which in many cases could reflect lower quality.

Additionally, rather than give you the measurements in degrees needed for your rebar angles, I felt it would be easier to provide you with a template instead. Oftentimes using a measuring device to decipher degrees can be a bit challenging. If you follow the instructions I set out for you on how to use this template, later discussed in Step 4: BENDING YOUR REBAR, I am confident you will find it to be effective and very simple.

NOTES

Rebar Angle Template

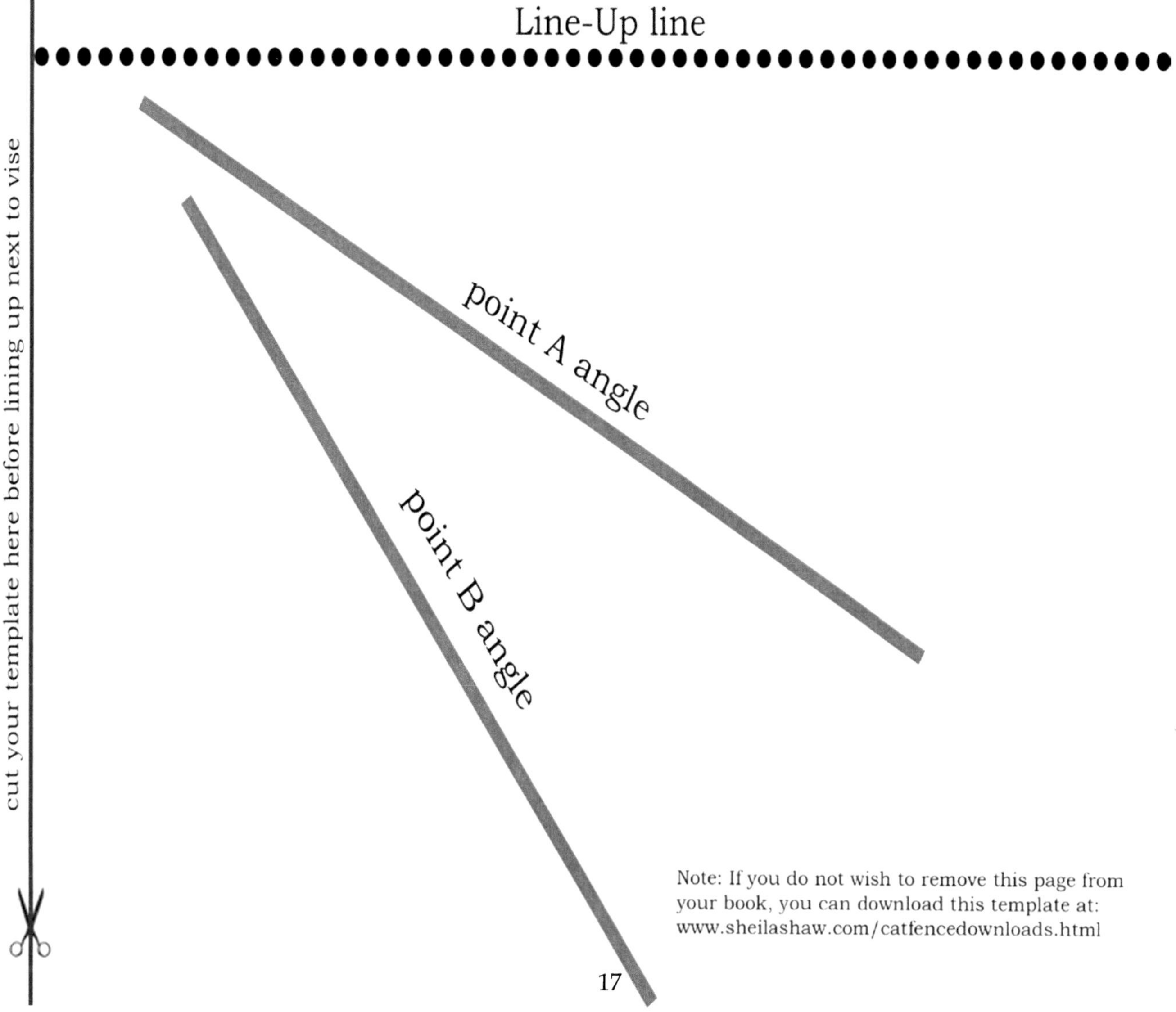

Line-Up line

•••

point A angle

point B angle

cut your template here before lining up next to vise

Note: If you do not wish to remove this page from your book, you can download this template at: www.sheilashaw.com/catfencedownloads.html

NOTES

✔	#	TOOL	USE	AVERAGE COST
	1	*Cutting* Pliers	Cutting fencing and zip ties	$15
	2	*Sledge*hammer 3lb min	Pounding the post	$16
	3	*Corded* Drill	Drilling post	$30
	4	*Vise* Grips	Putting rebar in post	$10
	5	Ladder 6′ min	Pounding the stakes & placing rebar	$35
	6	⅜″ x 16″ drill bit (*extra-long*)	Drilling post	$5
	7	Vise	Holding post & bending rebar	$25
	8	Tape Measure min 12′	Measuring rebar & post	$10
	9	Straight Edge	Marking rebar; *anything straight will work*	N/A
	10	Lumber Crayon in Yellow	Marking rebar; a white/yellow crayon will work	$2
	11	Ear Plugs	When drilling and pounding	$3
	12	Eye Protection	Eye protection	$4
	13	Gloves	Hand protection	$10
	14	Adult Helper	Placing the fencing and pounding stakes	Hopefully free!
		*The items listed below are **optional***		
	15	Post cap 1½″ or 2″	Protection for pounding post	$6
	16	Pouch	Carry zip ties and cutting pliers	$15
	17	Paint for rebar	Protective coating to prevent rust	$6
	18	Marking Paint	Marking post and post location	$6
	19	Rotary Tool & Grinding Bit	Grinding teeth from post cap	$20
	20	Spray Lubricant 3 oz WD-40	Placing rebar in the stakes	$2

#1 #2 #3 #4 #6 #7 #15 #16

#18 #19

Note: Many of the listed tools you may be familiar with. However, here are a few tools I felt an image could be helpful. Additionally, feel free to improvise many of the listed tools. Example: If you do not have a pair of cutting pliers and do not wish to purchase a pair, a pair of sharp scissors will suffice. Just keep in mind this list was put together with great care and you will need everything listed unless otherwise stated.

✔	TOOL	USE	AVERAGE COST
	Shovel	Digging post holes	$5 - $25
	⅛″ Drill Bit	Pre drilling gate screw or nail holes	$10
	Saw	Cutting 2x3s	$12
	Phillips Screwdriver or Drill Tip	Screwing in screws when securing 2x3s together	$3
	Level 9″	Checking posts are standing straight up	$10

If you will be building a gate(s), below is a list of additional tools you will need:

NOTES

Step 1 ASSESS YOUR PROJECT

Building a cat fence can vary in many ways as two are rarely the same. However, the process and materials will be. This is largely due to your desires and space, which will most definitely be different and unique. What I am offering you in this book is a definite plan to follow. However, the most important aspect is to know what you are up against before buying your supplies. Also, you might consider checking with your local building authorities to see if a permit is required. Additionally, if you will be constructing a fence that could be a potential issue with a neighbor, you might consider informing them on what your plans are.

During your walk-through you will be noting any and all obstacles, such as any trees you will need to go around, how large of an area you will be enclosing, as well as how you will be closing your fence. Example: Will you be tying into an existing gate or will you be building a new gate?

Tip: Keep in mind, cats don't like to jump over things; they like to jump onto things (flat surfaces), so LOOK OUT FOR THE TREES! If you build your fence as I am suggesting, I am confident your cats will not breach your fence; however, their means of escape will be low roof lines and trees! Consider these areas closely during your walk-through.

Note: If you run across a situation that appears to be a problem, oftentimes if you push on and then come back to it, the solution will be obvious. In other words, don't get stuck!

Before moving forward, I recommend you skip ahead to the DVD and select "TOUR." This is perhaps the most important section of the DVD because it gives you a glimpse as to what my challenges were and how I addressed them at the time. This can give you an idea of what to expect on your walk-through.

Step 2 GATHERING YOUR MATERIALS

If you have reached this point and you are committed to seeing the project through, now is the time to start gathering your materials and tools.

There are two options to build this fence—one using wood tree stakes and the other using metal stakes. In Step 6 PLACING YOUR REBAR I show you how to use either one. However, for now we will focus on the way I built my fence using "Tree Stakes, aka POSTS."

The first step is to determine how much material to purchase; avoid when possible purchasing more than you'll actually need. While I am a fan of not purchasing more than what is needed, with this project I did end up needing more rebar than I initially projected. If you are not sure, purchase a few more stakes and rebar and store them in a clean, dry area. This way, if they are not needed, you can return them, so be sure to KEEP ALL RECEIPTS!

Tree stakes, rebar, zip ties and deer fence pretty much sums it up.

Following are a description and the quantity of each that you will need.

✔	ITEM	DESCRIPTION / QUANTITY	AVERAGE COST
		Treated Tree Stake 2″ Round x 8′ Tall aka POST The size of the area you will be enclosing will determine how many stakes you will need. I set my stakes on average at 8′ apart.	$4.30 ea.
		Heavy Duty Deer Fencing 5′ - 7½′ x 330′ The size of the area which you will be enclosing will determine the amount of fencing. In my case I opted for 2 rolls of 6′ x 330′. A large quantity may be hard to get locally; be sure to order your fencing well in advance. **Note:** Do not use bird net to build your fence. You can use it as a roof guard as I did, but not as the main fence.	$210 - $274 eBay has great prices w / free shipping
		3/8″ x 4′ Steel Rebar For every post you will need a piece of rebar. In my case, I needed a few extra pieces for an existing fence and fence post. **Note:** 3/8″ x 4′ can be difficult to find. If this is your case, just purchase 20′ pieces and have it cut to 4′ lengths.	4′ length - $2.30ea. 20′ length - $4.30ea.
		Nylon Cable Ties aka Zip Ties 4″ and 8″ You will be using approx. three 8″ ties per pole. However, you will be using many 4″ ties for tying the fencing together. If my memory is correct I only needed one pack of each. The larger the area, the more of everything you will need.	4″ 100pk - $4.30 8″ 100pk- $6.50

	ITEM	DESCRIPTION / QUANTITY	AVERAGE COST
		If you will be building a gate(s), below is a list of additional materials you will need:	
✔	2x3x8 Wood Studs	Building the gate *(5 per gate)*	$2 ea.
	4x4x8 Fence Post	End post for supporting the gate *(2 per gate)*	$10 ea.
	Hinge	Securing gate to post *(2 per gate)*	$5 ea.
	Latch	Keeping gate closed *(1 per gate)*	$5 ea.
	Ready Mix / Concrete	Setting your post *(see recommended video)*	$4 ea.
	Screws or Nails	Securing 2x3s together (handful)	$2

Note: I used regular untreated white wood for my 2x3x8 and they are holding up great after 4 winters. However, choosing Redwood will assure longevity, but you will need to switch to 2x4s instead of 2x3s. Most local lumber yards will not stock 2x3s in Redwood. Either one will work, so do not worry about the difference in size.

NOTES

Step 3 DRILLING YOUR POSTS

Tools: *Vise, 3/8" x 16" drill bit, corded drill, post, eye protection and gloves*

For video tutorial refer to the DVD and select "POST/REBAR 1." In this section you will see complete instructions on how to accomplish this task. But please read this entire section first.

Once you have determined the amount of posts your project requires, I recommend drilling the holes in all of them before moving to the next task. Since you may have many, as I did, I also recommend if possible to do this indoors (garage). It is very important that when drilling your post you are in a comfortable environment away from excessive heat or cold weather. I say this because you must drill the holes straight/level and deep. This process can be time consuming; therefore good lighting and a comfortable environment will be helpful. This holds especially true for bending the rebar.

Since the drill bit is the same diameter as the rebar, placing the rebar can be a bit snug as it was in my case. However, in hindsight, I recommend making the hole slightly larger using the *same* bit. After you have completely drilled the hole, go back with the drill and wiggle it a *tiny* bit as you are drilling. This will increase the size of the hole, but be careful not to make the hole too large; you want the rebar to be snug. Having a sample piece of rebar near to test the hole diameter is a good idea. However, do not attempt to put the rebar all the way in at this time as you want to preserve the integrity of the hole until it is time to place the rebar.

Note: If you make your holes too large it can cause the rebar to swivel freely when you are placing the fencing, making it difficult to control.

Step 1: Secure your post in the vise and set your drill depth to **11 inches**. Make sure the post stays secure and level throughout the drilling process. It is important the rebar is solid and stays in place; therefore, your holes will need to be deep.

Tip: Wrapping a piece of colored tape on your drill bit at the desired depth will help assure your depth is correct and consistent throughout your posts.

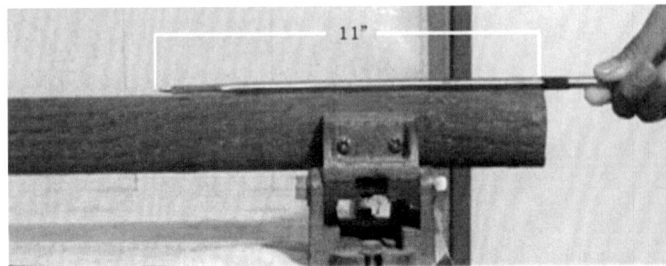

Step 2: Using a corded drill will give you enough power to drill your posts. It is important that you keep the drill level to avoid the drill bit from going in at an angle. This is very important so take your time and pay attention to your drilling technique.

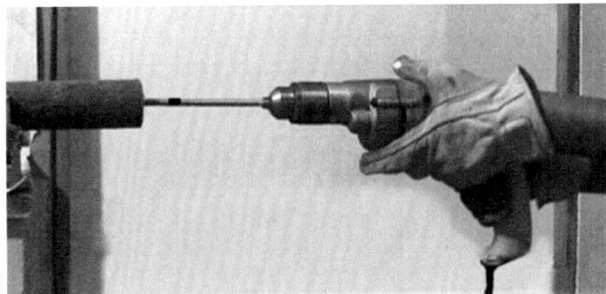

Step 4 BENDING YOUR REBAR

Tools: *Vise, 3/8" x 4' rebar, rebar angle template, eye protection and gloves*

For video tutorial refer to the DVD and select "POST/REBAR 1." Advance to 1:08. In this section you will see complete instructions on how to accomplish this task. But please read this entire section first.

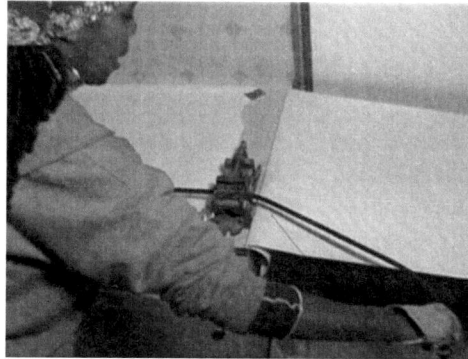

When bending your rebar it is important to understand what purpose the angle serves. If you have ever observed your cats climbing, you will notice they tend to favor climbing versus jumping. However, I don't want to be misunderstood, cats are awesome jumpers but I have noticed climbing appears to be their preference. They tend to stand at the bottom, look up and then proceed. This is where the angle of your rebar plays its very important role. When the cat looks up he/she will see there is no way to climb up and over. It is important your rebar is bent to create an overhang; otherwise, your fence may not work. It's the overhang the rebar creates that discourages your cats from climbing the fence. So let's begin!

Step 1: You will be making two bends in your rebar and both bends require different angles. First we need to mark our rebar in the appropriate places. From left to right measure 17", which will represent point A, and make a mark as shown below. Do the same on the opposite end of the rebar and measure 15"; this will represent point B. I suggest marking as many pieces as you can at once. This will be a great timesaver.

Step 2: Place your Rebar Angle Template on the right side edge of your vise. Line up your template by first placing a piece of rebar in the vise and close the clamp. Place the template "line-up" line where it is just below the rebar and then tape it down to avoid moving once you start bending.

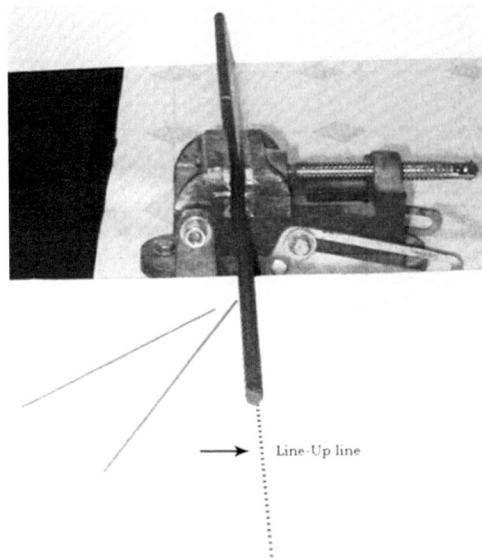

Line-Up line

Step 3: Once you have marked all of your rebar, we will begin the bending process. Place one piece of rebar in the vise with Point A at the far right edge of the vise clamp. This is where the first bend will occur.

Step 4: Pull the rebar towards you until you match it with Point A on your Rebar Angle Template. Repeat this process for Point B.

Once you are done bending your rebar, you may want to apply a coat of exterior primer paint to help prevent rust in the future.

Tip: It is important to make your bends level with each other. Example: After you have made your first bend lay the rebar on the table and when you pick it up to make your second bend, be careful not to let the rebar twist in your hand. If the rebar is allowed to twist in your hand and you place it in the vise this way, your rebar will come out looking warped. This will not affect your fence; however, it will look crooked when you are placing your fencing on top.

Note: While the goal is to make your rebar pieces as uniform as possible, there is room for error. Try not to go crazy trying to match your rebar exactly to one another. The purpose of the rebar is to hold the fencing and create an angle, which I am confident you will accomplish if you use the "Rebar Angle Template" I have included. Many of my pieces were off by an inch or so and all was well!

NOTES

Step 5 SETTING YOUR POST

Tools: *Post, sledgehammer, straight edge, ladder, post cap, marking paint, eye protection and gloves*

For video tutorial refer to the DVD and select "POST/REBAR 2." In this section you will see complete instructions on how to accomplish this task. But please read this entire section first.

Setting your posts by far will be the most physically challenging. Not only must you wield a 3-pound sledgehammer while balancing at heights of 6' plus, but you must also have a doggone good aim to boot! Having hindsight is the mother of all wisdom. If I knew then what I know now, this process would have been a lot easier. Good news for you!

Okay, first off you will notice in the DVD I was using a 1½" galvanized pipe cap (which I refer to as "post cap") to protect the top of my posts. The problem was I did not know this item would come in so handy until I was already in the middle of the post-setting process and had to run out and find something quick to avoid losing the great momentum I was gaining. I went to two different hardware stores and could only find a 1½" when a 1¾" or 2" would have been a lot better. Additionally, while writing this book I wanted to offer a better cap and found a 2" at OSH, which I will discuss later in this chapter.

But for now I do want to say that while testing the new size cap, we just had a huge storm two days prior and the ground was PERFECT for pounding posts!

Wow, even though I did attempt to soak my posts it was still in the middle of July. If I had to redo this process, I would definitely plan setting my posts after a good HEAVY rain. The process was like night and day.

I do want to mention, however, if planning this project around a heavy rain is not an option, definitely resort to the initial plan and soak the posts and even consider doing this a few days in a row to be sure the water is able to soak deep or at least 10"-16". With that being said, let's get started.

Step 1: Determine how deep you will set your posts and then mark them. When I was planning my fence I contacted a fence builder (not cat fence) and explained what I was doing. He said that I should set my posts 24" and then went on to say if I did not go this deep, my fence would fall down within 6 months! Here it is 5 years later and my fence is standing strong and I only went down 10". In my DVD I initially said I would go down 18", then 16" and finally settled on 10". At this point I was thinking about what the builder said and was unsure. However, now I am sure. My recommendation would be to set your posts between 10" and 16" and this should be just fine. If you have really soft soil, choose the latter and go a bit deeper.

Note: If you set your posts too deep, you can jeopardize the height of your fence and render it useless. While cats are climbers, they are great jumpers too! Also, once your posts are tied together with the fencing, it will add tremendous strength and stability.

Step 2: With all your posts marked to the correct depth, now determine where your posts will go. This is largely determined by how large of an area you will be enclosing. My project was quite large; therefore, I set my posts approximately 8 feet apart. I say approximately because there were quite a few scenarios where a tree for instance would be at the 8-foot mark and I would usually opt to go over the mark versus under. My average was between 8 and 9 feet apart and this has worked very well. However, there are some instances where I have a cluster of posts; for example, around my gates. Additionally, while the goal is to have your fence the same height, for me this was an impossible task as my yard is very uneven with many slopes, so do your best to keep the height.

Tip: Do the best you can with what you have to work with.

Note: Using marking paint is great for marking the location as it is bright and easy to see. Also, if you are working with someone who is unfamiliar with the process, this will come in handy. Just instruct them to locate the orange marks and place a post there.

Step 3: Preparing your ground is very important and will make all the difference with what type of experience you will have while setting your posts. Once you have your post locations, place a post at each location. Set the post approximately 4″ in the ground and with a garden hose soak the area at the post hole. Repeat this process over a few days so when you are ready to set your desired depth this will go a bit easier.

Step 4: Pounding your post is a delicate process. It is important to remember the first 11″ of your post will be at a slightly compromised state due to the holes you have drilled. Your post will succumb to many blows from the hammer; therefore, taking extra precautions to protect your post top should be of high concern. It wasn't until I was already underway with this task that I realized how important it is to protect your posts.

While this is not a requirement to get this job done, I highly recommend using a "post cap" as described in your list of tools. Not only did the cap serve as a protector, but I was able to really pound the post and the metal cap added force to my strikes and drove the post in easier.

At the time I only had a 1½" post cap available, which was a bit challenging to work with. However, I have since found a 2" cap. Using the 2" cap is not totally without its setbacks. While the post is marked at 2" in diameter, the true measurement is approximately 1¾", which adds a bit of a wiggle when the cap is hit since the cap is ¼" larger than the post. After a few swings, you may need to center the cap again. However, I found this to be very effective and not at all too inconvenient when considering the alternative.

Tip: If I had to do this process again, I would opt for the 1½" cap if a 1¾" was not available. I would purchase a *few* of them and ground the inside teeth out before I got started on the project. If this is an option for you, I recommend doing this; it will make all the difference.

Note: Keep in mind, it is not altogether necessary to use a post cap. People have been driving posts in for years with nothing protecting them and no harm done! However, if the top (holes) are damaged, it will be hard to go back and repair once the posts are in the ground.

Step 6 PLACING YOUR REBAR

Tools: *Rebar, vise grips, ladder, spray lubricant, sledge or large hammer, eye protection and gloves*

For video tutorial refer to the DVD and select "POST/REBAR 2." Advance to 6:55. In this section you will see complete instructions on how to accomplish this task. But please read this entire section first.

Placing your rebar on your posts is an exciting point to be at for two reasons; first, you will be able to see your fence taking shape and second, you are almost done!

Step 1: Grip the rebar with the vise grips a few inches below point A. Be sure to position your vise grip in a comfortable position for you to hold when you start pounding. How snug your holes are will determine how tight you will need to clamp the vise grips. If you do not clamp your vise grips on tight, when pounding, the vise grips will slip down the rebar versus the rebar slipping down the hole.

Tip: Applying a thin coat of spray lube will help the rebar slip down the hole; it will also allow the vise grips to slip down the rebar, so try not to spray any lubricant where you clamp the vise grips. Spray your lubricant on after you have securely applied the vise grips to avoid this from happening.

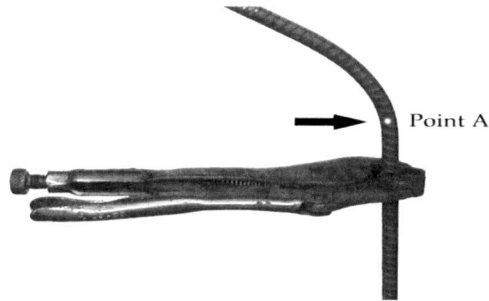

Point A

Step 2: With the vise grips clamped on the rebar, place the rebar in the post hole with the rebar facing forward and begin to pound the rebar down. How much force you will need to accomplish this will depend on how snug your holes are.

Tip: Pay close attention to keeping your rebar facing forward and not sideways when pounding it in. This can be overlooked since you will be focusing primarily on getting the rebar in the hole and not so much on the direction your rebar is facing. If you do not pound your rebar straight it can be hard trying to correct it after it has been pounded in the hole.

Note: Your hole is only 11" deep; therefore, keep this in mind to avoid over pounding. Additionally, the size of the hammer needed will depend on how snug your rebar is.

Alternative: USING METAL STAKES

Using metal stakes is another way to build your fence. I chose not to use this method simply because it would cost me $150 more and I had a very specific budget. However, if you'd rather use the metal stakes, below is what you will need and how to use them. You will be following all the same steps except skipping Step 3 DRILLING YOUR POST.

Note: The metal stakes drive into the ground a bit easier; therefore, you may not need to soak your ground as much. Additionally, when pounding, you will not need the post cap for protection.

✔	ITEM	DESCRIPTION / QUANTITY	AVERAGE COST
		8 ft. Steel T-Post The size area you will be enclosing will determine how many stakes you will need. I set my stakes on average at 8' apart.	$7
		Steel Bed Frame Rail Clamp You will need one clamp per post.	$3 ea. 2pk

Step 1: You will need to make a slight modification to the clamp to fit the odd-shaped post. Place the clamp in your vise or use a hammer and close the gap until the clamp will slip onto the post without falling off.

Step 2: Once you have adjusted all of your clamps and with your post in place, you can now place your rebar on top. First place the clamp on the post and then slide your rebar between the clamp and post. Set your rebar down approximately 9"– 11" from the top.

Tip: Using your vise grips to hold the rebar in place will leave both hands free to adjust and tighten the clamp. Additionally, your clamp will need to be tight; for extra strength use a pair of pliers.

Step 7 BUILDING YOUR GATE(S)

Tools: *Shovel, cutting pliers, saw, drill & bit, level, phillips screwdriver or hammer, eye protection and gloves*

If you will not be adding a gate(s), skip this section and proceed to Step 8.

The focus in this book is guiding you with building a cat fence and not a gate. However, if you will be adding gate(s) to your project, I would like to offer you a brief tutorial on how to accomplish this task. While this tutorial is a basic overview on how to build a *simple* gate, I am confident if you follow the step-by-step instructions, you will have no problem completing this task successfully.

Tip: YouTube offers a variety of videos focusing on how to build a gate. If you need more instructions, go to YouTube.com and search "How to Build a Gate."

Note: I do want to add that this was not my primary gate as shown in the DVD. I have a main gate preceding both of my "cat gates."

Step 1: Before you begin to build your gate, I recommend setting the gate posts first. The width of your posts will determine how wide you want your gate. When deciding, consider what you will want to go through it (wheelbarrow, garbage, etc.). Once your posts are in place and set, build the frame to match the posts.

Here is a great two-minute video on how to set your post. Copy this link in the address bar of your browser to access this video. http://www.quikrete.com/athome/Video-Setting-Posts.asp

How to Set Posts

Tip: You will be placing a piece of rebar at the top of each post. Drill the holes for your rebar <u>before</u> you set the posts. If you miss this step, it will be difficult but not impossible to add them later. Additionally, be sure your posts are level before the concrete sets. Your gate will function much better when it is straight and square.

Note: Working with concrete can be intimidating; however, do not let this discourage you from moving forward. If you follow the simple instructions in the video, you will be just fine. Keep going; you will be glad you did!

Step 2: Place a 2x4 at the top inside of the post. If you place the 2x4 on top of the post, be sure not to cover the holes you drilled for the rebar.

Tip: You can do this step before the posts set; this will help you square your posts.

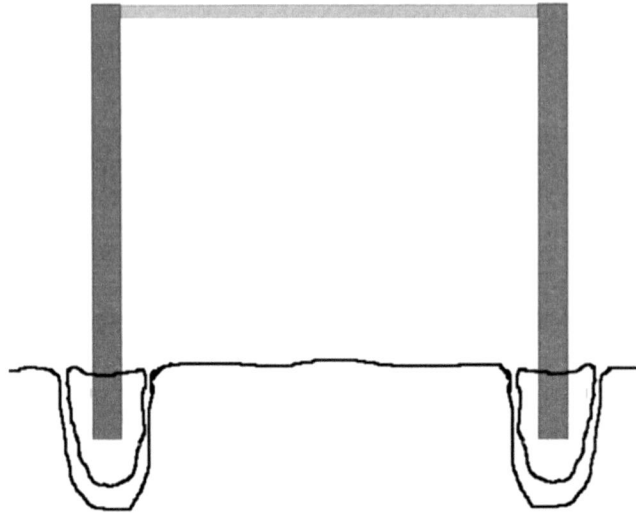

Step 3: Assemble your gate. Make your gate's final width 1½" - 2" narrower than the actual <u>inside</u> post width. You will be wrapping your fencing around the post and gate; therefore, you will need the extra room.

When assembling your gate, lay your 2x3s flat on the ground and square them up as much as possible. Be sure to match your 2x3s on both sides. Example: When building the gate, if you place the top 2x3 on the inside of the left 2x3, be sure to do the same on the right side. If you do not do this, your final measurement will be altered from your initial desired width.

.

Tip: Assemble all 4 sides before placing the final center 2x3. The center 2x3 is what gives your gate stability and strength. Additionally, predrilling your screw or nail holes will prevent your wood from splitting when pounding your nails or screwing in your screws.

Note: The width of your gate may vary depending on how level you placed your posts. If your posts were not set level, the top width can vary from the bottom. This will determine how square you will want to make your gate. Remember, your gate will need to fit between your posts.

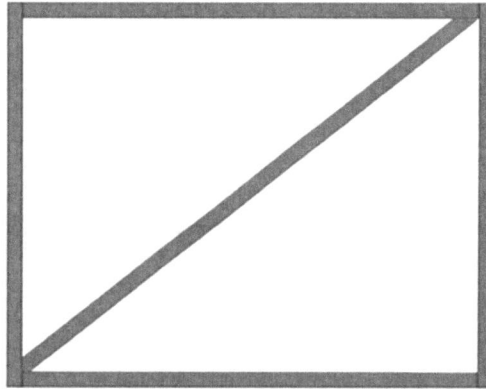

Step 4: Attach your gate to your post using gate hinges. Place your hinges approximately 15" from the top and bottom of your posts.

Tip: Do not place the fencing on the gate until after you have tested it to make sure the gate fits and functions properly. You will need to remove the gate to put the fencing on and then re-hang it on the post.

Note: If the ground below is not level, it could keep your gate from swinging open. You may not have room to adjust the gate. Therefore, you will need to remove some dirt to allow the fence to swing open fully. Be careful not to remove too much dirt, as you do not want the cats going under the gate.

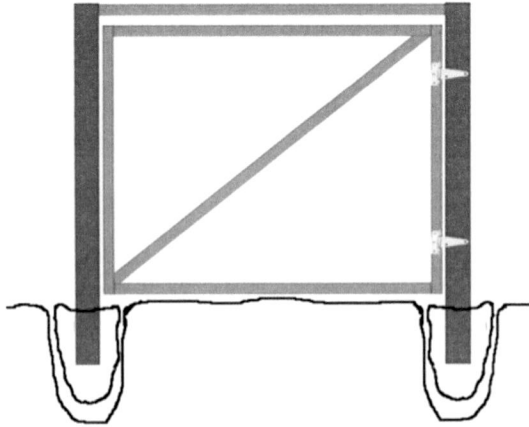

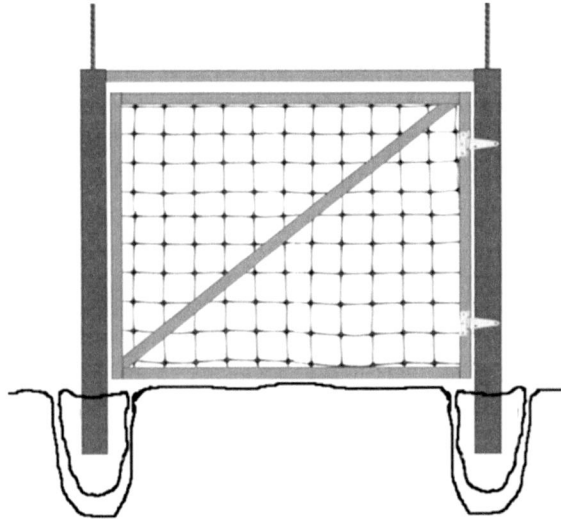

Step 8 PLACING YOUR FENCING

Tools: *Fencing, pouch, cutting pliers, zip ties, ladder, eye protection and gloves*

For a visual on how this is done, refer to the DVD and select "FENCING."

Placing your fencing will require the help of an adult helper.

Step 1: Place your fencing roll at one end of your project and unroll enough to allow you to slip the fencing above and over your rebar. The top layer of your fencing should be behind your post and rebar. Once you have done this, using a 4" zip tie, tie the fencing to the tip of the rebar to secure it in place. You may want to place another zip tie in between point A & B as well. Before placing your 8" zip tie on the post, you will want to unroll enough fencing to cover the span of 4-5 posts. By doing this, you will be sure your fencing is straight and not crooked.

Tip: Try to make one continuous piece with your fencing. For now, only use the 4" ties to secure the fencing to the rebar. To avoid having to go back and straighten the fencing, keep watch that you are putting it on level throughout the span of your posts before completely securing it.

Step 2: Once you have the top of your fencing in place, using another piece of fencing, place it in front of the posts on the bottom half of the posts. You will be creating a barrier at the bottom, so overlap the fencing on the ground at least 12".

Tip: Do not secure the fencing to the posts using the 8" zip ties yet. For now, use the 4" zip ties to secure the fencing together. Until you are sure your fencing is level only place a few zip ties every several feet.

Step 3: Once all of your fencing is in place, go back and secure your fencing to your posts using the 8" zip ties. Additionally, secure all areas where the fencing is overlapped using your 4" zip ties and place them every 12".

Note: There is no specific amount of zip ties to use; use as many as you feel necessary to secure your fencing.

STEP 9 CREATING YOUR BARRIER

Tools: *Gloves, eye protection*

The barrier of your fencing is important and serves two purposes: 1) keeps your cats from digging out of the yard, and 2) keeps other critters from digging into your yard.

Note: When I was building my fence you will see I used roofing material and brick for my barrier. However, I want to note at the time I did not know I would have the opportunity to use the brick. In hindsight, I do not recommend using the roofing material.

Step 1: Use whatever materials available to place on top of the fencing that was overlapped at the bottom of your posts. Anything heavy will work—planks, logs, bricks, rocks, etc.

Tip: Do not use gravel; it is not heavy enough.

PRECAUTIONS

Once you have completed your fence, it is a good idea not to let the cats out during stormy weather. If a tree falls on your fence, it can possibly breach your fence letting your cat(s) free to the world during a storm. Additionally, it is a good idea to do frequent head checks. If your cat(s) do find a way out of your yard, it will be hard for them to get back in, leaving them locked out.

FREQUENTLY ASKED QUESTIONS

Any territorial issues? Before the fence went up, my cats all had their favorite areas in the yard and it has carried over. It seems they still favor their chosen areas and they do not overlap with one another. My yard is large, offering them enough space to call their own. So the answer is no, I have not had any issues regarding territory.

Predators getting locked in the yard? Initially, soon after the fence was built, a few raccoons would still pop in occasionally. They would climb down the trees and into the yard. However, that was short-lived and I have not seen or heard a raccoon in the yard for years. However, I want to add for the first year, I would not allow my cats in the yard all night due to the fact a raccoon could be in the yard. Now skunks are a different issue. Amazingly, skunks have tiny bodies and can squeeze through the fencing and do show up in the yard occasionally. I am not as threatened by skunks because the only harm they cause is a foul smell, whereas a raccoon can and will kill a cat.

Poles coming out of the ground? No, none of my poles have ever come out of the ground. Actually, it has been just the opposite. As time has passed, the poles are even stronger now than when initially set. The fencing adds to the stability and keeps the posts secure.

How often do you check your fence for breaches?

Initially, after the fence was completed, I checked it a few times during the day. Because I had never built anything to confine cats, I was not sure if it would work or not. As time passed, I relaxed a little and started doing a walk-through approximately once a week or when I was doing yard work. However, I want to note no matter how much time has passed, it is a good idea to make it a habit to check your fence for breaches regularly. It is important to remember for the cats that used to go outside your yard, this will be a drastic change for them and they will never (at least in my case) stop wanting to explore their "old stomping grounds"!

FOOD FOR THOUGHT

If a (healthy) cat stops eating, oftentimes a change of feeding location is all that is needed. One day as I was feeding my cats, I noticed Casey would not eat. Of course my first assumption was she did not like what was being served. After a few days and 3 different cat foods later and no change, I got a notion to just move her food dish. Oddly enough, I moved her dish no more than 12 inches from where it was and she began to eat! Try it and see.

If your cat does not sleep in his/her bed or cat condo anymore, move it! Similar to moving the cat food, I noticed none of my cats would sit in the cat condo on my deck anymore. No matter what I did — changed the blanket, vacuumed it — they just would have nothing to do with it. So I decided to move it to the other side of the deck and sure enough, it became a favorite slumber platform again.

If your cat suddenly stops sleeping on their favorite blanket/bedding try washing it. One day I noticed my beautiful Zoe was sitting beside her blanket. I could not understand this behavior. So I would pick her up (as if she could not do this herself) and I would place her on the blanket. No sooner would I put her there than she would return to the spot beside the blanket. After a few days, it finally dawned on me to change/clean the blanket and sure enough, she got on the blanket and went to sleep. This may sound like a no-brainer; however, I do want to emphasize, her blanket, at least to me, did not smell nor did it appear to be soiled. But from her point of view it needed changing! Side note: Avoid using any cleansers that have heavy fragrance, as this can be irritating to our four-legged friends.

The floor is the closest thing to our animals. For many of us shampooing our carpets or cleaning our hardwood floors is an absolute must, especially when you share your palace with your four-legged friends. However, we often overlook the floor is the closest thing to our animals; therefore, any chemicals we use come in direct contact with them. Before I wised up and removed my carpet, I would use hot water to clean my carpet and it removed 90% of the stains. I should note most of my stains were dirt and the occasional regurgitated food, if you know what I mean. Try it, it's amazing what hot water and a good mop or shampooer can do on its own. If you do need assistance from a chemical, only use it on the area in question rather than on the entire floor.

Aggressive behavior. Before sending your pet packing, consider changing their food first. I know this may sound a bit curious; however, let me share with you how I discovered this behavior relating to food. Niles, one of my cats, became an absolute nightmare, I mean, "timeout" was his middle name. I say "became" because he was not always this way. He was a very sweet and gentle cat, and his behavior took a drastic turn. He became aggressive towards everyone just for looking at him. I could not understand this behavior. However, I am a bit embarrassed to admit it, but I remember every time he would eat, he would vomit. This is not when it dawned on me to change his food. Unfortunately, it wasn't until much later when my grandmother's cats had to move in.

Gremlin had food allergies and needed special food. Rather than feeding her separately, I swapped out my cats' food and upgraded to a grain-and-gluten-free diet for everyone, and this is when Niles's behavior drastically changed. I mean it was drastic and what seemed to be overnight. Not only did his aggressive behavior change but he was no longer vomiting his food.

After doing research on food allergies and food intolerance, I learned oftentimes food allergies/intolerance may not be obvious and can develop over time, such as in Niles's case.

Additionally, aggressive behavior can also be attributed toward a toothache or other hidden ailment. My sister-in-law had a similar experience with her dog Jazzers, aka Tasmania Devil; she was an absolute nightmare. She snipped at everyone and barked all the time. It turned out she had a bad tooth and once it was fixed her behavior improved.

RECOVER YOUR LOST PET USING STRATEGIC SIGN PLACEMENT

For video tutorial refer to the DVD and select "BONUS." In this 20-minute instructional bonus section, you will learn from start to finish how to make your signs. You are shown my neighborhood and where I placed the signs, as well as examples of what not to do with your signs. I am confident after viewing this tutorial, you will always be well armed whether you are looking for your lost pet or assisting another.

Note: In order to fully convey the importance of strategic sign placement, I would like to engage you with the story of Cherry, the missing Chihuahua.

If you have heard it once you will hear it again: NOTHING IS IMPOSSIBLE!

My best friend, Peggi, often teases me, stating, "Sheila, you need a cape like Batman's, but instead it should say Pet's Pride since you are always quick to aid in the safe return of a lost animal." I always laugh at this but she is right. I can't help myself. If I see animals that even look like they are missing, I will stop whatever I am doing and see if they are in need. I have rescued many animals, including Buster the Dachshund, another story worth telling; Bogey, a beautiful white Samoyed; two Afghan hounds we later named Mufasa and

Simba; Boogie, my own cat missing for 4 days; Kali, a Chocolate Lab; and many more. And while all of them have left a lasting impression on me, it's Cherry's story that truly holds a special place in my heart. Her story is so unique and magical it deserves to be told in detail.

On October 9th, 2012, a friend and I were enjoying one of those beautiful rare sunny days that come far in between when you live in a forest next to the ocean. While sunny days do occur, oftentimes, while beautiful we experience fog and chilly days more often than I care to experience as I climb up in age.

As we slumbered on my deck, having a bite to eat and totally caught in a euphoric state of bliss sucking in the vitamin D the sun offers, and with the birds chirping as if to add their gratitude for the sunshine, and with all of my animals surrounding us, this was destined to be a day I would remember for the rest of my life. As we both sat back and sank even deeper in the lounge chairs we were slumbering in, all of a sudden we were blasted out of our state of ease with an immediate sound of what seemed to be a very vicious dog fight involving a human, as the dog growls were intertwined with loud squeals of a human voice.

Oh my gosh! We flung out of our chairs and determined the fight was directly behind us and on the other side of the back lot my property abuts. My cat fence prevented us from running through the lot so we jumped in my car and zipped around the corner to find my neighbor, Lilly, standing in the street totally stressed, as she was wrestling her two dogs that were fighting each other. This was definitely a case where their bark was bigger than their bite as neither one of them suffered any injuries, nor did Lilly.

However, there was a third dog, her tiny 6-month-old Chihuahua puppy, Cherry, who was frightened by all the ruckus and darted down the street, and the more she was chased the faster she ran. As Lilly explained what happened, she could barely speak as she was shaken from the fresh experience that sent adrenaline rushing in her veins accompanied by sick worry with Cherry on the run. Little did I know from this moment on Lilly and I would forge a bond that would last a lifetime from the journey we would soon take together over the next four days. At this time it was unbeknownst to us it would take another 96 hours to reel this little whippersnapper in.

With Cherry so tiny, keeping an eye on her whereabouts as she dashed was almost impossible. She blended in with just about everything, fallen trees, pine cones and the forest floor too!

Compelled to help, we took a few spins around the block to see if we could spot her. I had already gotten Lilly's phone number just in case. After a few turns around the block I had no choice but to retreat home as I was already late for an appointment. I checked in with Lilly a few hours later to see if she had recovered Cherry and she said no! I explained I would help her but needed to go to class as I was right in the middle of finals. I called Lilly again after class, about 8:30, and still no Cherry. I explained to Lilly she needed to put signs up and she assured me she would.

At this point, now completely dark, cold and damp, everyone had given up and claimed Cherry lost forever. After all, she had no jacket, no food; she was in HEAT and alone with all the predators that come with the forest night—owls, raccoons, mountain lions, foxes and whatever else. With these thoughts riddling through my mind I put my heaviest coat on, grabbed a flashlight and continued to look for her until midnight. I too was now sick with worry.

The next morning I called Lilly and she was so upset she could hardly speak. I knew she was in no shape to put signs up and at this point what she needed was a hero. So I grabbed my invisible cape and went to work. Since I own a laminate machine there was no need for me to run to the local office supply to have signs made. I had Lilly send me a picture of Cherry and with that made about 20 signs as well as leaflets. I used a very specific strategy when placing the signs, which I detail in the section "BONUS" on the DVD. At this point I was completely committed. After placing all the signs and delivering the leaflet fliers to Lilly I returned home for work and told Lilly I would join her in a few hours. This was the juice Lilly needed; now armed with fliers, she walked the neighborhood streets talking to people and giving them a leaflet.

Soon after the fliers went up, she began to receive calls stating Cherry had been spotted. Oh my gosh, I can't tell you how exciting this was. SHE WAS STILL ALIVE!!!! After a few hours had passed and once free from obligations, I joined Lilly on the hunt. We looked for hours, took a food break and continued. People were calling but no one could catch this little ball of fire. Whenever someone would call we would immediately go to that area and start looking. Once again as the night set in we had no choice but to surrender the search until the next day.

On the third day I had a feeling this would be the day we would find Cherry. Again I had to leave Lilly for a few hours and return later after free from my obligations. Convinced this was the golden day, I called my professor and explained what was going on and asked if he would allow me to take my final exam on another day; he agreed. However, if he had not, I was willing to miss the final altogether because Lilly needed my help and I was not going to leave her stranded. I was the only one involved who was offering hope as the others had given up and expected Lilly to follow suit.

After an hour or so passed we got a call stating Cherry was in the next town over about four miles down the road. WHAT? This was shocking and a bit hard to believe. However, the person was completely convinced based on the description in the flier so we immediately went and posted new fliers and again the calls were pouring in. We were so excited and knew it was only a matter of time. And then the worst thing that could possibly happen, happened. It started to rain, and I mean pour, and the night fog swept in fast! Lilly and I walked for hours in the pouring rain calling Cherry, and finally around 10 p.m. once again we were forced to surrender. All the excitement we had built up soon turned into a deep feeling of defeat.

The next morning came long and slow as we both were unable to sleep. Unfortunately, since I had rescheduled my final exam and I didn't think my professor would appreciate me requesting another day, I was obligated to take my exam that morning. I was so upset because I just knew we would find her and I knew Lilly was counting on my strength, but what she did not know was I was depending on hers as well. Around 11 a.m., after I completed my exam, I checked my phone just in case Lilly called and sure enough there on my phone at exactly at 10 a.m. was a message stating in a very emotional voice, "Sheila, I found her ALIVE!" So while she was finding Cherry I was acing my exam. She then went on to explain Cherry was sitting under a shrub and at first started to dart away before realizing it was Lilly and then dashed in her arms. Lilly told me she almost did not get out of bed that morning fearful she would never see Cherry again, but she had an overwhelming hunch she should go look one more time.

I was so elated I felt as though I was floating 10 feet off the ground. I was jumping up and down trying very hard to constrain myself. Keep in mind I was still in my classroom, but luckily, it was only me and my professor in there at the time and even as I tell this story I can feel the joy within me as if it were happening all over again. This was such a magical experience it is engrained deep in my soul; wow, to be a part of such a success, for me, represents the crème de la crème of life.

This was truly the sweet smell of success. To this day I still have that message and suspect I will keep it forever.

On my way back from school I made the rounds collecting all the fliers so Lilly could just rest and reunite with her puppy. Who would have thought that not only could this puppy survive the elements that were at hand, but her little 4-inch-long legs could get her four miles down the road to boot.

I'm often asked what compels me to drop my life for the welfare of a missing animal and honestly, outside of my deep love for animals, I just simply want to be the person who would look for my pets should they go missing.

After a few days had passed Lilly brought Cherry over as I had never met her, and boy, what a little ball of MIGHT she is. You talk about feisty; no wonder no one could catch her!

Unless you have sufficient proof your missing pet will not be returning, keep your signs up and never give up faith.

When all was said and done, I have one regret. I wish we would have placed an ad in the local paper letting everyone know she was safe at home. There were so many people who responded to the signs and they deserved to share in the success of her recovery. Perhaps they will read this story.

Please share this story so everyone who may have lost a pet or know of someone who has can take comfort in knowing you can recover your pet, even when it seems impossible. This story is available for sharing, along with the tutorial video, at: www.sheilashaw.com/catfencedownloads.html. *Like it, Facebook it, Share it!*

Sincerely,

Sheila Shaw